Ready to Learn
Treasure Hunt

How To Play

1 Press the Power button to turn the SD-X Reader on or off. The LED will light up when the SD-X Reader is on.

2 Touch the volume buttons found on this page to adjust the volume.

3 Touch words and pictures on the page to hear audio. These icons start the following activities:

 Hear the story.

 Hear the word.

Spell the word.

 Play a game.

4 After two minutes of inactivity, the SD-X Reader will beep and go to sleep.

5 If the batteries are low, the SD-X Reader will beep twice and the LED will start blinking. Replace the batteries by following the instructions on the next page. The SD-X Reader uses two AAA batteries.

6 To use headphones or earbuds, plug them into the headphone jack on the SD-X Reader.

Volume

Publications International, Ltd.

SD·X INTERACTIVE

Battery Information
Includes two replaceable AAA batteries (UM-4 or LR03).

Battery Installation
1. Open battery door with small flat-head or Phillips screwdriver.
2. Install new batteries according to +/- polarity. If batteries are not installed properly, the device will not function.
3. Replace battery door; secure with small screw.

Battery Safety
Batteries must be replaced by adults only. Properly dispose of used batteries. See battery manufacturer for disposal recommendations. Do not dispose of batteries in fire; batteries may explode or leak. Do not mix alkaline, standard (carbon-zinc), or rechargeable (nickel-cadmium) batteries. Do not mix old and new batteries. Only recommended batteries of the same or equivalent type should be used. Remove weakened or dead batteries. Never short-circuit the supply terminals. Non-rechargeable batteries are not to be recharged. Do not use rechargeable batteries. If batteries are swallowed, in the USA, promptly see a doctor and have the doctor phone 1-202-625-3333 collect. In other countries, have the doctor call your local poison control center. This product uses 2 AAA batteries (2 X 1.5V = 3.0 V). Use batteries of the same or equivalent type as recommended. The supply terminals are not to be short-circuited. Batteries should be changed when sounds mix, distort, or become otherwise unintelligible as batteries weaken. The electrostatic discharge may interfere with the sound module. If this occurs, please simply restart the sound module by pressing any key.

In Europe, the dustbin symbol indicates that batteries, rechargeable batteries, button cells, battery packs, and similar materials must not be discarded in household waste. Batteries containing hazardous substances are harmful to the environment and to health. Please help to protect the environment from health risks by telling your children to dispose of batteries properly and by taking batteries to local collection points. Batteries handled in this manner are safely recycled.

Warning: Changes or modifications to this unit not expressly approved by the party responsible for compliance could void the user's authority to operate the equipment.

NOTE: This equipment has been tested and found to comply with the limits for a Class B digital device, pursuant to Part 15 of the FCC Rules. These limits are designed to provide reasonable protection against harmful interference in a residential installation. This equipment generates, uses, and can radiate radio frequency energy and, if not installed and used in accordance with the instructions, may cause harmful interference to radio communications. However, there is no guarantee that interference will not occur in a particular installation. If this equipment does cause harmful interference to radio or television reception, which can be determined by turning the equipment off and on, the user is encouraged to try to correct the interference by one or more of the following measures: Reorient or relocate the receiving antenna. Increase the separation between the equipment and receiver. Connect the equipment into an outlet on a circuit different from that to which the receiver is connected. Consult the dealer or an experienced radio TV technician for help.

Writer: Brandon Myers

Cover illustrated by Olin Kidd

Illustrator: Olin Kidd

Louis Weber, C.E.O., Publications International, Ltd.
7373 North Cicero Avenue   Ground Floor, 59 Gloucester Place
Lincolnwood, Illinois 60712   London W1U 8JJ

Customer Service:
1-888-724-0144 or customer_service@pilbooks.com
www.pilbooks.com

SD-X Interactive is a registered trademark in the United States and Canada.

Manufactured in China.

8 7 6 5 4 3 2 1
ISBN-10: 1-4508-4678-5
ISBN-13: 978-1-4508-4678-3

Monkey has a lot to do. He has to mow the grass. He has to clean the house and wash the towels. He has to paint his wagon. And carrots must be planted in the garden too!

"How will I ever finish?" Monkey thinks.

Someone knocks on the door.
Elephant is here.

"Let's go to Owl's house,"
Elephant says. "He wants to
show us his treasure map."

"I wish I could, but I have to
mow and clean and wash and
paint. And after that I have to
plant carrots!"

"I will mow and clean. You can wash and paint," Elephant says. "We'll plant carrots last. If we share the work, we'll finish soon."

Monkey nods. "I like your plan. We'll have time to go to Owl's house."

Elephant mows the grass.
Monkey washes the towels. He
hangs them on the line to dry.

Elephant cleans the house.
Monkey paints his wagon. "We
can quit soon!" Monkey says.

"Here are the seeds," Monkey says. "I'll start at this end of the garden."

"I'll start at the other end. Let's meet in the middle," Elephant says.

Monkey and Elephant use all the seeds. The garden is finally planted.

"Thank you for helping me, Elephant. Now we can go see our friend Owl."

"Go start the engine. I will bring our helmets," Elephant says.

Monkey and Elephant zoom down the road. They stop to talk to Walrus in the park. Walrus is sleeping.

"Wake up and join us, Walrus! We are going to see Owl," Monkey says.

"I would rather stay and nap," Walrus yawns.

Monkey and Elephant drive through town. They see Giraffe. Giraffe waves to them.

"I am going to the office. I am too busy to play today," she calls.

Monkey and Elephant drive out of town. They drive past orchards and fields. "Summer is the best time of year," Monkey says. "Look at that rainbow!"

"I agree," Elephant says. "Look at that big, red barn. And I see a horse eating flowers!"

The Treasure Map

Monkey and Elephant arrive at Owl's house.

"Come in and look at my map," Owl says. "I received it from my uncle. It came in the mail yesterday."

Elephant jumps up and down. "Let's go on a treasure hunt!"

"That's a great idea," Monkey says. "I think I would enjoy that."

"Let's read the words on the map," Owl says.

"There is a fort on Ivy Island. Let's sail there and look for the key," Elephant says.

Monkey, Elephant, and Owl
sail across the lake to Ivy Island.
Monkey jumps out and sees
a sign.

"The arrow points that way, but
ivy is blocking the road."

"I will make a path," Elephant
says.

They follow Elephant up the road. The fort is on a hill. Monkey notices something shiny at the top of the fort.

"Look up there," he says. "Is that a key?"

"I think it is," Elephant says. "Can you reach it, Owl?"

Owl flies to the top of the fort. He reaches for the key. "I have it! I will toss it to you, Elephant," he says.

"Now let's try to open the fort," Elephant says.

Elephant enters the fort first.
"I see a rope!" he says.

"Hmm, something about rope was written on the map," Monkey says.

"Yes!" Owl says. "Climb the rope and look for a letter."

Monkey climbs the rope and finds a letter. He opens the letter and reads it. "I think this letter offers hints."

Travel to the jungle on the road going west.

A nail in a branch keeps the mail in the nest.

"Hmm, what should we do now?" Monkey asks.

"Let's follow the hints," Owl says.

Monkey, Elephant, and Owl travel to the jungle. They see a road through the trees.

"This road goes west," Elephant says. "Let's walk along it and look for a nest."

Owl looks up high, but he only
sees vines and branches.
Elephant looks down low, but
he only sees flowers and grass.
Monkey notices something on a
branch. It looks like a nest.
Monkey leaps onto the branch.
"I found a nest!" he yells.

"Do you see a nail?" Owl asks.

"Or any mail?" Elephant asks.

"Yes!" Monkey says. "A nail keeps the mail in the nest."

Monkey tosses down the mail and Owl catches it. Owl opens the mail and reads the letter.

Look in the log under the nest, if you wish to find the treasure chest.

"Look in the log under the nest," Owl says. "Do you see anything?"

"I see a square box made of wood," Elephant says.

"It must be the treasure chest!" Monkey says. "Open it, Elephant!"

Elephant opens the chest...

The treasure chest is filled with gems
that twinkle blue and red.

Monkey finds a golden crown
and wears it on his head.

Owl counts all the silver coins
and makes three equal stacks.

Elephant divides the rest
and gives each friend two sacks.